Hell Night" by John Barcus

Chapter 1 "The Base"

Jake walked away from his parent's house on Mitchell Drive down Stonewall Drive. Jake's hair was half way down his back, and was beginning to shift from blonde to red, as the fall shifted to winter. Tonight was October 30th, Hell Night.

Jake had just gotten permission to stay overnight with his friends Joe, and Rob. The sun was already slipping down the Eastern sky. Jake's lanky figure cast a long shadow on the broken, and faded black top street. Jake's long blonde, and red hair blew in the wind like flames, as he walked up the street.

Jake paused for a moment at the intersection of Cleaborne Drive, and Stonewall Drive. Jake stopped and considered the Northwest corner of the intersection, as he stood in the middle of the street.

Jake pulled a pack of Marlboro reds out of his red flannel shirt pocket. He shook a bent, and flattened cigarette out of the soft pack. The pack had been in the side of his sock all day, while he was at Thurman Francis Jr. High School.

Jake put the cigarette in his mouth and struck a match, and inhaled the smoke. He watched the flame flare up from the cigarette as he let his breath out. He took a deep lung full of smoke.

Jake leered at the Northwest corner of the street, where a year ago, he had been nearly pummeled to death in front of his parents, as they watched helplessly.

Jake blew the smoke out, as he began to walk up the street. Sewart Airbase was a rough place, the worst. Jake only knew it as "The Base", a government housing project on the outskirts of town.

"The Base" had been built in 1941, as officer housing during World War II. It was decommissioned in 1971 and made into low income housing. Ten years later it had decayed to its present state.

"The Base" was a dangerous place and Jake, like most, who lived here, learned that lesson that hard way. The base was ruled by various drug dealers, and warlords. Jake had proved himself a potent adversary to anyone on many occasions, but there was always the possibility of getting jumped.

Jake walked down the middle of the street. His long blonde, auburn hair blew in the autumn breeze. Jake wore a black Led Zeppelin t-shirt under his red, flannel shirt. The black decaying concrete crumbled under his red Chuck Taylors. His jeans were nearly faded white and were frayed, and torn at the knees.

Jake appraised the empty corridors between the red brick houses. If Jake heard a car behind him he would quickly move over the crumbling curb, and onto the sidewalk. The drivers in this neighborhood would try to run anyone over. Jake had no idea what made people so vicious and crazy here. If you lived here, your senses had to be keen. Jake continued walking down the middle of the street. It was safer. If you walked out on the sidewalk, you could be attacked by someone lurching out from between the houses. No matter how good you were in a scrap, you had to be ready and had to be able to see a trap before it was sprung.

Jake passed Carter Street. He observed a vacant house on the left side of Stonewall Drive with the windows broken out. He and a girl had snuck into the house last month at night to get high, and have sex. The was another house on the right, that had mostly burned down about a year ago. Vines covered the house, and tall weeds grew in the yard.

Jake's cool, light blue eyes casted upon the corner of Grandberry Drive and Stonewall Drive, where the bus had dropped him off not thirty minutes before. Jake had seen many vicious fights at the bus stop in the morning, before school. He had seen Tony Owens knocked out three times by a wrestler named Trey Benton, before Tony pulled a knife and stabbed Troy.

Jake had a few minor skirmishes at the bus stop last year, while he was in seventh grade. Since then Jake had become a serious student of whatever pieces of martial arts he could pick up off the street. What he learned he practiced diligently. You could never know enough and Jake had become known from his brutal street and backyard sparring matches. Even at 13 years old, 5', 10' and at a lanky one hundred pounds, Jake was becoming known as a fast and formidable fighter.

Jake rounded the corner of Stonewall. On the left lived a kid two years older than Jake, and they were at the early stages of an awkward, kind of frenemy relationship. The kids name was Garth Yates. Across the street lived Garth's cousins, The Owens brothers, Tony, and Darren.

 Tony was Jake's age, but he was very athletically developed for a boy of 13, and was as competent a streetfighter as any adult, who lived on The Base. Tony's brother Darren was a year younger, but physically developed beyond his years. The survival of the fittest nature of The Base grew men into boys before their time.

As Jake rounded the corner Joe was standing in the front yard smoking a cigarette. Joe was nearly a man himself at sixteen. Joe was tall, lean, and Jake thought he resembled Dan Aykroyd. Jake considered this in his mind, Joe's brother Rob also resembled Dan Aykroyd, so did their mom. The whole god damn family resembled Dan Aykroyd more than they rightfully should have.

Joe smiled at Jake with a cigarette hanging out the side of his mouth and laughed. Joe and Bob were the only real friends Jake had in this whole neighborhood, the whole world really.

"Boy, you better get off the streets, before somebody kicks your ass!" Joe shouted, as Jake smiled back.

"Boy! Boy? Fifteen pounds of swinging meat!" Jake recited, as he pretended to hold an elephant's trunk sized dick between his legs.

 "Balls the size of watermelons!" Jake mimed holding his titanic testicles, as he leaned forward, straining his back.

"Enough hair on my ass to weave a rug!" Jake said, as he turned, as he walked backwards pointing with both hands at his narrow ass.

Jake spun around and held his hands to the heavens in disbelief.

"And you're still calling me 'BOY'?!?" Jake finished.

Joe shook his head, and laughed, as Jake stepped up into Joe's yard.

"So what is up, Jakey boy?" Joe asked.

"Couldn't say. Don't know. What is on the itinerary?" Jake asked.

"Well, step inside my lair." Joe said, waving his hand toward the door of his home.

"Thank you, sir" Jake said, as both Joe and Jake flicked their cigarettes simultaneously into the yard's dry, dead grass and walked into Joe's house.

Chapter 2 "Concoctions"

Joe led Jake into Joe's and Rob's home. Joe's mother was sitting in the disorder of the living room. She was wearing a dirty, white house coat with rose patterns on it. She wore glasses and her hair was dirty and oily.

"Hello, Miss., Mrs., Ms. Frack?" Jake stammered, not sure of their mother's marital status.

"Ellen.", Ellen answered. She appraised Jake with a world weary and worn face. Exactly how old this lady was was hard for Jake to discern.

If you wanted to have sex with a burned out lady in her forties, who looked like Dan Aykroyd, Ellen Frack would be your first choice, Jake thought to himself.

"Hi, I am Jake Baker, your son's friend.", Jake offered.

Ellen Frack stared at Jake with a cynical and amused expression, as she drew on her cigarette.

"Thank you for allowing me to stay over.", Jake added.

"So are you going to terrorize the neighborhood with Joe and Rob?", Ellen asked flatly.

"I...", Jake stopped, and looked to Joe, who was smirking at Ellen's and Jake's exchange.

"Jake is going to cure cancer, feed the starving in Africa, and bring peace to the Middle East, Ellen.", Joe wryly offered.

Ellen rolled her eyes.

'What the fuck ever.", Ellen said, and got up, straightened her housecoat and walked to the kitchen.

Jake surveyed the room.   The Frack house was full of clutter. Books, clothes, cartons of cigarettes, clothes, film canisters, magazines, novels, record album covers, Playboy magazines, dozens of TV Guides were piled on the furniture and the carpet. Some of the random items were junk, however some of the items and furniture were expensive.

Joe had shared the family's story with Jake. Ellen Frack had lived in the New England area and had married a wealthy man. At one point the family lived in a big mansion. Apparently her husband's insane children and wife had made him leave for ice cream and he kept going. How the Frack family landed on The Base Jake did not recall. They had family around here or some shit, Jake vaguely recalled Joe saying?

I guess like Miss Havisham, Ellen' Frack's life went badly and she said, Fuck it, Jake thought sadly.

"Come with me.", Joe put his hand on Jake's back, and guided him into the hallway.

"The mad scientist is hard at work.", Joe said.

"Rob is a scientist?", Jake asked.

Joe laughed, opening up Joe's and Rob's bedroom door.

"Rob is a Scientologist." Joe replied.

"Fuck you.", Rob replied with a cigarette dangling from the corner of his mouth.

Rob was sitting in a wooden chair with an old dining table sitting in front of him. Rob was fifteen. He was slightly shorter than Joe. Rob had brown hair, whereas Joe had blonde hair. It was clear they were brothers, and likely the illegitimate children of Dan Aykroyd, Jake thought.

Rob was focused on pouring something from a coffee can into a funnel stuck in a bottle.

Jake looked at Rob and the clutter on the table. There was a bottle of bleach, several different colored bottles of dye, a box of lye, several metal containers with corrosive warning labels on them, a metal container labelled "hydrochloric acid", a few cans of oil enamel paint, a container of kerosene and a can of gasoline beside Rob. Jake's eyes widened as Rob drew on his cigarette, pulled it from his mouth, and flicked ashes on the floor beside himself.

Joe observed Jake's reaction and chuckled. Joe stood silently regarding his brother Rob with a swell of pride.

Jake looked to Joe, who smiled at Jake.

"So how are you there, Rob?", Jake asked Rob,

Rob intensely focused on the work before him, poured two, or three different chemicals into his mixing can.

"What are you doing there, Rob?", Jake asked bemused.

"Well Jake, my man... I am making some concoctions.", Rob replied off hand.

"Little 'eye of newt, and toe of frog, Wool of bat, and tongue of dog'...touch of death strangled baby?" Jake asked apprehensively.

"Not going to blow us up like the Hindenburg?" Jake continued.

"Working here, people." Rob replied in a voice of focused concentration.

Jake surveyed the floor of the brother's bedroom and for the first time noticed dozens of glass soda bottles with paper labels taped to them with yellow masking tape. The labels read "Green face", "Straw Head", "White out", "Blister Juice", "Oh Fuck!", "Ha! Ha!", "Mace Perfume", "Burn, Witch, Burn!"...

Jake looked from the bottles back to Rob as Rob poured his mixture of doom into a half full, glass Sprite bottle. The liquid in the bottle began to bubble and smoke.

Rob drew on his cigarette, and looked at the bottle.

"Oh, oh.", Rob said cautiously.

Smoke began to billow from the bottle. Jake took a step back toward the door to the hallway. Behind Jake, Joe laughed and took the bedroom door knob into his hand.

"Nope, nope, nope!" Rob said to the bottle, as he picked it up, and dropped it into a plastic bucket of ice and water sitting beside him.

Jake heard a sizzling sound, as steam rose from the bucket and the water in the bucket boiled. The ice water bubbled for a few more moments, then stopped.

Rob waved his hand in the air. "Wow. Hot, hot, hot." Rob said around his cigarette.

Rob took the cigarette from his lips, then flicked its ashes into the bucket. Rob picked up a plastic container of dish soap, the box of lye, and began to tap the lye into the coffee can.

Jake hyper-focused on Rob now asked, "So what is a...?" Jake considered and bit his lip. "What does...do these...?", Jake began to ask Rob.

"Working!" Rob said, beginning to pour some bleach, and more dish soap into his mixture.

"Come on, Jakey." Joe laughed and put his hand on Jake's shoulder. Joe opened the door and led Jake into the hallway, then shut the door.

Jake stepped quickly down the hallway to the living room.

Amused, Joe followed behind Jake at a leisurely pace.

"Hungry, Jake?", Joe asked.

Jake shook his head. "More worried about dying than hungry.", Jake replied.

Joe laughed. "I am going to make some biscuits and tea." Joe offered.

"Have a seat." Joe pointed to one of the chairs at the kitchen table.

"Sure." Jake said.

Jake shook a cigarette from his pack.

Last one, Jake thought.

Jake considered the cigarette for a moment as he looked back toward Joe's, and Rob's bedroom.
Jake shook his head, pictured himself running into the street on fire, then lit the cigarette.

Joe threw ten tea bags into a large pan on the stove, filled it with water, turned the gas flame on the stove, then placed the pan on the burner.

Jake looked around.

"Where is your mom?", Jake asked.

"She probably went to visit the neighbors.", Joe replied, as he opened the refrigerator.

Joe grabbed a container of biscuit dough and popped it on the counter.

Jake jumped at the sound.

Joe began to lay the biscuits out on a baking pan and he turned on the oven.

Jake looked around the house. All the houses on The Base, were duplexes, and were laid out as mirror opposites to each other. Beside the kitchen was the back door.

Exit in case of sudden explosions, Jake thought to himself.

Beside the door was a washer and dryer.

"Sugar, or milk?", Joe asked, bringing Jake out of his daze. Joe was holding Jake's hot tea.

"Just sugar. Lots of sugar. It goes great with a cigarette.", Jake said.

"Jake, you are an odd bird." Joe said, pouring sugar into Jake's tea, then handing Jake a spoon.

Joe sat down at the table across from Jake.

"Tell me about these concoctions?", Jake asked Joe.

Joe laughed to himself for a moment.

"Well Jake, Rob makes them every year for Hell Night." Joe began.

Jake also had another question about Hell Night. Jake knew it was an invitation to wanton destruction, but Jake had another question. Jake often hung out with older people, because they knew things that Jake was curious about. However, when Jake hung out with people like the Frack brothers, he knew he did so at his own peril.

"The concoctions do a variety of things. Rob threw one on Seth Rizzo last year and it turned his hair green and his parents had to shave his head.", Joe said, laughing as he pictured Seth's bald head.

"Rob dumped another one on a kid's pants, and it blistered his legs. The kid had to come out of his pants. He ran six blocks home and his parents had to spray him down with the garden hose." Joe sipped his tea and shook his head laughing.

"Fucking hell? Did they turn Rob into the police?" Jake asked, wide eyed and wondering what kind of shit he was about to step into alongside these maniacs.

"Sure, but my mother just told the police Rob didn't live here anymore.", Joe chuckled.

"The police let it go like that?", Jake asked incredulously.

Joe smirked. "Sure, what else could they do?"

Jake blinked at Joe. Jake knew his father would have kicked his ass in if he did some shit like that.

"Then Rob dumped a concoction into a little kid's trick or treat bag and melted the kid's candy, then burnt a hole in his bag." Joe said slapping his knee.

"The fuck?", Jake replied.

The Base kids often threw away any handmade, baked goods or anything not factory sealed. Last year, a ten year old tripped for three days on some candy laced with LSD. Kids often smashed candy before eating it to make sure there were no tacks or needles in the chocolate or gum.

Jake was worried about what Joe and Rob were talking about doing. Jake did not mind engaging in some harmless pranks, but what Jake saw here could land a kid in jail and make him enemies with some cruel and vindictive people.

Then Jake considered the possibility that he might be able to mitigate some of the Frack brothers' more destructive intentions. Jake sometimes was able to be the voice of reason in this hellish and mad neighborhood.

Joe watched emotion play across Jake's face, as Joe laughed silently to himself.

Joe watched as Jake mouthed the word "Okay." silently and unbeknownst to himself.

Jake looked up at Joe and said, "Joe, can you tell me a few things about Hell Night, please?"

"Like what, Jake, my man?" Joe asked.

"Like…" Jake began.

Chapter 3 "Hell Night"

According to Manuel Roig-Franzia, a writer for The Washington Post explains in his article "The Mischievous History of Devil's Night". Devil's Night, similar to it's Southern twin, Hell Night, occurs on October 30th. It is a night, when people engage in acts of vandalism, arson, alongside more innocent pranks as eggings, soaping windows, or leaving a flaming bag of animal feces on a doorstep. The practice was known as early as the 1940s, but came more popular in the 1970s to the 1980's in such cities as Detroit, Michigan, and other inner city, and high crime neighborhoods, like Sewart Airbase in Smyrna, Tennessee.

Joe explained to Jake that in the Northeastern city, where the Fracks had lived near Devil's Night was a night when neighborhoods burned. Joe said since he and Rob had lived on The Base they had participated in the mayhem of Hell Night.

"Last year," Joe explained to Jake, "Robbo and I pissed off a good many people, especially the Owen brothers. Hell Night is not just a night of random destruction, it is a chance to fuck with all the people who don't like us." Joe said, biting into a burnt biscuit.

Jake considered Joe's phrase "all the people that don't like us" and thought, THAT is no short list, but nodded to Joe that he understood.

"Hell Night is also a night for pay back to all the people who fucks with us." Joe said laughing.

"But it is also a night that anyone you pissed off gets their payback on you." Joe said and nodded at Jake.

Jake's stomach churned at the thought of all the people he might have pissed off. Jake considered all he had said and done to upset anyone in the last year. Jake knew there were people, who simply when looking for trouble here on The Base. People, who beat people up just because they were fucked up on speed and were in a hostile mood. There were kids, who had gotten abuse by their parents, so likewise they found a random kid, and took their frustrations out on them with their fists. There were guys who wanted to improve their street reputation, so they found someone smaller, weaker or unprepared and beat the living hell out of them. There were guys and women who were always looking for some slight to use as an excuse to pummel the fuck out of someone. Jake realized if he thought about it he could come up with a reason why anyone he knew might want to physically attack him. On the streets where there was no money violence was currency and gave one status.

Hell Night, as Joe described it, sounded like a recipe for disaster to Jake. Jake was learning to control himself through practiced violence. Jake was no expert of violence, but he knew that without good judgement and heroic self control, violence, like one of Rob's dangerous concoctions, though intended for someone else, was likely to spill back on its user and have crippling or lethal results.

Jake knew his friends, both Joe and Rob lacked good judgement or self control, infact they were fucking maniacs. But Jake knew there was no hiding or running from violence, mayhem or insanity on the dangerous streets of The Base. Jake had tried to hide and avoid these things, but no matter what he did, violence, mayhem and insanity found him. Because those things existed, not just on the streets, but inside Jake's home and in himself. The best thing one could do is become as competent as possible at dealing with violence, mayhem and insanity.   And the only way to do that was to begin.

Jake's face was pale and his hands were cold, but he looked at Joe with his cool, blue eyes and said, "Okay."

"Are you good with this?" Joe asked.

"No, not all of it." Jake said with trepidation.

"Are you going to snitch on us?" Joe asked, more as an admonition than a question.

"No." Jake answered earnestly.

"Good, because I will kick your ass if you do." Joe said.

Jake considered this. Joe was bigger than Jake and had a few years experience on him, but Jake seriously doubted Joe could win a fight against him, but he let it go.

"I hear you." Jake answered.

"So, Jakey boy, let's get you set up." Joe said, returning to his jovial tone.

"Sure." Jake answered.

Joe led Jake into the Frack's cluttered living room and pulled a large pair of shears from the drawer of a coffee table.

Chapter 4 "The Three Shaolin"

Joe dug into the pile of clutter and found a box full of bolts of brown and black silky cloth. Rob came into the living room from the brothers' bedroom.

"Alright." Bobby said and assumed a faux kung fu stance.

"Okay, Jake my man. Come here." Joe said to Jake.

Jake walked over and Joe held up a bolt of brown cloth and began to roll it out.

"How tall are you?" Joe asked Jake.

"About five ten, I think." Jake replied.

Joe began to let out double the length that he had measured Jake with a single sheet.

"Hey, give me one of those bolts, Joebo!" Rob said to Joe.

Joe reached into the box, snagged a bolt of ocher colored cloth and threw it at Rob, hitting him in the face.

Rob tried to catch the bolt before it fell to the floor, but missed. Rob picked up the bolt and said, "You will never pitch for the Yankee's, fuck stick."

Joe and Jake laughed at Rob's comment.

Joe cut a hole in the brown cloth for Jake's head, then clipped a large black square from the black cloth and made Jake a short cape to top off his robe. Next Joe cut three long strips of cloth from the black bolt.

"Here put your head through this." Joe instructed Jake.

"What the hell is this?" Jake asked as he did as Joe instructed.

"We are going to be disguised as Shaolin priests tonight." Joe answered.

"Ahhhh, yes Master Po." Jake replied.

Jake slid the black mini cape over his head, then Joe handed Jake the long black strip of cloth.

"What do I do with this?" Jake asked Joe.

"It is your sash. You tie it around your waist." Joe answered.

"Congratulations Jakey boy, you are now a black belt." Bob quibbed, as he worked on his Shaolin priest costume with a lit cigarette hanging from his mouth.

"Gee whiz, I always wanted to be a black belt." Jake beamed

"As the headmaster of the Frack Temple, I declare you a black belt of asshole Kung Fu." Joe said, as Joe tied Jake's belt in two single knots at his waist line.

"I always wanted to be declared an asshole." Jake joked.

"You could not have found a more qualified mentor." Rob said.

Joe laughed.

"Now Jake, there are a few things I need to bring you up to speed on." Rob said working on his robe.

"Like what?" Jake asked.

"Like the police that will be on the look out for people fucking shit up, but to be specific me, us, Joe, and I." Rob said.

Jake silently mouthed, "And I", then said"Okay." to Rob.

"Buuut especially me, because I have active warrants out on me." Rob continued.

Jake thought about asking what the warrants, plural with an "S" were for, then realized the warrants were not for him, and they were not Rob's point... probably not.

Joe removed a burnt sienna cloth from the box and went to work making his costume.

"So you want to be on the lookout for the paddy wagons. They will be going around picking people up and taking them to jail, because after 11pm it is after curfew for minors." Rob said.

"Besides, you are wanted by the police." Jake paused, then asked," What is a 'paddy wagon'"? as he looked around the room.

"A paddy wagon is a big police truck they throw your ass into, before they take you to jail." Rob replied.

"Yes, stay the fuck away from paddy wagons." Joe concurred.

"Paddy wagons?" Plural? With an 'S'?" Jake said apprehensively.

"I thought The Base was outside city limits, so all we had to deal with was the retired base cops, who can barely bring themselves to give a fuck." Jake said exasperated.

"The Base is, but tonight is special. Because all of the arson, vandalism, assault and fuckery, the county police and state patrol are brought in." Joe said, finishing up his costume.

Jake and his friends frequently ran from the part time, semi retired, and indifferent pseudo police after flipping them off, calling them "pigs!", shooting their trucks with bottle rockets, or roman candles, or hurling eggs, and bricks at them. In fact, Jake like most Base kids, had mastered the art of eluding the police by age thirteen. They had a million strategies. Sometimes the fleeing kids would cut through the backyards in the middle of the block. The police would race them to the otherside of the block to cut them off, but the sly kids would just double back, leaving the furious cop on the other side of the block holding his dick.

The Base kids knew all the hiding places, sheds, vacant houses, fields with tall weeds, wooded areas, and if all that failed, there was always a friendly grown up on every block that hated the police, who would let a kid hideout in their house, until the heat was off. But even considering all that, what Joe and Rob were telling Jake gave him serious pause.

"Now if the police do catch you, DO NOT give them your name." Rob warned.

"Or yours either?" Jake stated.

"Not unless you want to be charged with first degree assault, breaking and entering and vandalism." Rob replied.

"And first degree rape of the neighbor's chihuahua." Joe added laughing.

"Fuck you, that dog was asking for it." Rob retorted.

Jake looked from Rob to Joe bewildered then asked. "Is that true?"

"No, Jake." Rob huffed in frustration, then jeered, "Fuck you." as Joe and Jake laughed.

"So you did infact rape a tiny dog?" Jake asked wryly.

Joe fell on the floor laughing.

Rob threw a pack of Winston Light cigarettes at Jake. Jake blocked his face from the cigarette pack and the pack of cigarettes fell to the floor. Jake picked up the cigarette pack and removed one from the pack and threw the pack of cigarettes back to Rob.

"Now can you throw a lighter at me?" Jake requested.

Rob, finishing up his costume, fished a lighter from his pocket and tossed it to Jake. Jake caught it deftly, then lit his cigarette.

"Hey man, can I get a light off that?" Joe said, asking for the lighter, while shaking a cigarette from his pack of Winston regulars.

"Sure." Jake said and tossed Joe the lighter. Joe lit his cigarette, sat down in his costume on top of the clutter on the couch, then slipped Rob's lighter into his pocket.

"Hey fuck wad! Give me my lighter back!" Rob jeered at Joe, as Rob started to slip his robe over his head.

"Sure, but that is Mister Fuck Wad." Joe laughed and hurled the lighter at Rob's crotch as hard as he could. The lighter contacted Rob's balls.

"Ow! Goddamn!" Rob screamed, as he fell to the floor and doubled over.

Joe broke into laughter, as Jake tried to stifle his laughs.

Jake, not wanting to sit on the clutter on the furniture, found an empty spot on the floor, and sat down cross legged. Rob pulled his head through the hole in the robe, and put his mini cape over it.

"Now one more thing Jake." Joe said.

Jacked looked at Joe and listened.

"If the police catch you, especially if they have to chase you, they are going to bring an ass kicking." Joe said with a voice of experienced authority.

Jake considered all the people who were likely to beat up him and the Frack Brothers tonight.

Jake looked from Rob to Joe and asked, "Is there anyone on The Base tonight, that does not want to kick our asses?"

Rob lit a cigarette and looked at Joe. Joe looked back at his brother. Rob and Joe paused for a moment, then turned their heads to Jake, shook their heads and said "No."

Chapter 5 "Into The Darkness"

Joe handed Jake a red 1/38 inch thick, fluted drape pole.

"Here you go, grasshopper." Joe said.

For a thing that was made to hang drapes off of, you could not have asked for a more practical and ornate weapon.

"Thanks." Jake replied.

Jake marvelled at the drape rod for a moment.

Rob was wearing a pair of cargo pants and in the many pockets he was putting various concoctions.

Jake thought, Rob, if you fall on the street and bust four or five of those biological weapons you are going to be reduced to a human slug.

Jake shook his head and shivered at the thought, then comforted himself by realizing like the many warrants on Rob's head, the concoctions were NOT Jake's problem.

If Rob broke those death sodas on himself and WHEN the police showed up, Jake wanted to be far, far AWAY!

"Code red, disavow." Jake said quietly to himself.

Joe watched silently amused by Jake's unawareness that he was processing his thoughts aloud.

Joe walked into the kitchen, opened the refrigerator, picked up a large fillet of white fish, and put it into a paper bag. Joe opened a cupboard, grabbed a bottle of lighter fluid and dropped it into the bag as well.

There were so many recipes for disaster present, that Jake could think of nothing to do, but wait to see how someone was going to die, or wait for something to blow up, or run away. ...or just wait to see how this chaos was going to manifest itself, he was going try to avoid getting as little as possible on him... that is if he planned to stay the night.

Jake heard Rob grunt under the strain of something. Jake turned to look to Rob. Rob was hefting a large bowling ball up to his chest with both hands.

"K.", Jake said silently.

"Yo, Joebo open the fucking, back door." Rob said, stumbling toward the back door.

Joe opened the door. Jake watched as Rob stumbled out the back door and launched the black ball over the patio into the pitch black, dark night. The ball landed in the grass with a heavy thud.

"God damn Rob, be quiet. Be cool, fool." Joe shushed Rob.

Rob simultaneously flipped Joe off and grabbed his dick, as he walked back into the Frack house and slammed the door.

"Jakey-boy, come here-sere" Rob said.

Jake walked over to Rob.

Rob handed Jake a hair tie.

"Jake, part of the purpose of our costume is a disguise. We, I, Joe, you do NOT want people to recognize us for obvious reasons." Rob said.

Jake silently processed this for a moment, then said "Because you don't want to be arrested, have your ass kicked in by the pigs, then get ass raped in jail?"

"Or murdered by rivals, or people I pissed off...." Rob waved his hand as if to wave away a fart.

"So tie your hair back into a ponytail, then put it into your shirt's collar." Rob continued.

Jake grabbed his hair, and wrapped the tie around it. Jake looked at Rob, then Joe. Though Jake's was tight against his head, Jake's hair still practically glowed with it's blonde and red color.

Rob shook his head and said, "No other guy on The Base has this colored hair! Everyone is going to know it is you the moment they see you."

"Take the hair tie off. It looks fucking ridiculous!" Joe jeered at Rob.

Jake grabbed the tie from his hair and handed it to Rob. Rob took it, looped it over his fingers, and drew it back with his other hand, and shot it at Joe.

Joe was writing something on a large white soft ball. The hair tie hit Joe in the ear.

"Stop, Fuck wad!" Joe warned Rob.

Rob flipped Joe off again. Jake walked over to Joe and read over Joe's shoulder what was written on the white, soft ball. Printed in black marker was written:

"Welcome to the neighborhood! On behalf of The Benevolent Sewart Airbase Welcoming Committee! WE LIKE YOU! "

Joe dropped the ball into the paper bag with the raw white fish and the lighter fluid. Rob walked to the back door, stopped next to Joe and Jake and waited.

"Ready?" Joe asked and looked to Rob then Jake.

"Sure." Jake said, feeling both excited, worried, as his stomach groaned.

"Affirmative." Rob answered with the mock authority of a special forces operative.

Joe opened the back door and the three priests of mayhem stepped into the darkness.

Chapter 6 "Smoke and Fire"

Jake walked beside Joe and Rob toward the open field behind the duplex. It was fully dark and the patio lights were out on the Frack's and their neighbors patio.

Suddenly Jake felt Joe grab the back of his shirt.

"Be careful Jake." Joe said, "Watch out for the clothes wires."

Until Joe said it, Jake did not see the rusted, metal clothes wire in the darkness. The clothes line posts were made of thick metal poles in a T form.

"They will take your head off." Rob whispered, then Joe shushed him..

Rob shushed Joe back.

Jake ducked under the clothes wires and watched Rob and Joe from some distance away in the darkness.

Rob walked up to the outside of his neighbor's dryer vent hood. Ducking under the dining room window, Joe and Rob crouched, as

Rob grabbed onto the metal vent hood, and slowly and carefully pulled it out.

Jake could hear the neighbor's dryer running.

As Rob removed the vent hood some dust and lint blew out in his face. Rob waved the dust away and he stifled a cough. Joe slapped Rob in the head and held his hand over Rob's mouth. Rob pulled the vent hood free as Joe giggled.

Joe reached into his brown, paper bag and pulled out the large, white fish fillet.

Joe slid it into the hole of the dryer vent. Rob picked up a broom leaning against the shed and used the handle to push the slimy fish into the dryer. There was a small clunk as the fish meat fell into the dryer on the other side of the wall.

Joe and Rob ducked down and Jake moved around the edge of Frack's shed and hid.

From the window above the dryer one of the two, neighbor sisters pulled back the yellowed curtain and peered from the window for a moment. Joe and Rob hunkered down and waited. If she came out the back door, Joe and Rob were busted.

Jake's heart beat hard for a moment, as he peered around the corner in dread. Then the sister drew the yellowed curtain back and left the window. Rob slid the vent hood back into the dryer vent hole.

Next Rob tore open the large, black trash bag sitting on the back patio. Joe reached into his own brown, paper bag and pulled out the yellow, plastic bottle of lighter fluid, shove his hand deep into the trash bag, then sprayed the fuel deep into the trash. Rob flicked his lighter and ignited some paper in the trash bag in two or three places.

As Jake watched he noticed the flames were rather small and he wondered if they might just go out on their own. Rob and Joe retreated from the neighbor's patio to where Jake was standing.

"Come on." Rob whispered to Jake.

Jake followed Rob and Joe into the dark field. The field was unkempt and weeds had grown almost four feet high. Joe, Rob and Jake skirted the Owen brother's house by twenty feet away.
Joe, Rob and Jake stopped on a tall, grass covered knoll on the West side of the duplex beside the Owen's house.

The boys kneeled down using the tall grass as cover. Joe and Rob peered at the house in front of them. It was only about nine o'clock but the lights were out in the house.

Jake remembered meeting the people who lived there. Joe and Rob had introduced Jake to the couple, who had recently moved to The Base from California. The man was in his thirties and the woman was in her fifties.

Jake could not remember if they were a couple, or mother and son. There was something unsettling about the couple, but Joe and Rob seemed friendly to them, so Jake wondered why Joe, Rob and himself were hiding out and spying on their house.

In the dim, Jake saw Joe remove the soft ball from his bag. Jake recalled the message Joe had written on the ball, "Welcome to the neighborhood! On behalf of The Benevolent Sewart Airbase Welcoming Committee! WE LIKE YOU! "

Joe looked over at Rob as Rob removed a concoction from his cargo pants.

Joe rose up, and drew his arm back like a pitcher winding up, then threw the soft ball. Jake heard the ball whiz through the air, then he heard it slam into the brick wall of the house then the ball came bouncing back across the field.

Jake expected the boys to bolt, but Joe and Rob held their ground, as Joe laughed.

"Fuck." Rob said quietly and laughed

Jake watched Joe and Rob to see what to do next. No lights came on in the house. Jake's pulse was racing. It was a cool fifty degrees that night, but sweat was breaking on Jake's forehead.

Joe stood up again, drew his arm back and took another throw. Jake heard the ball whistle through the air, then heard the kitchen window shatter.

Joe broke into devious laughter. Jake could not help, but laugh at the audacity and absurdity of these maniacs.

The light flicked on in the house's kitchen window. At that exact moment, Rob rose up to his feet and launched one of his glass, bottled concoctions. The bottle disappeared into the darkness for a moment, then the dining room window shattered. The house seemed to fill up almost instantly with thick, sickly yellow fog, which came billowing out of the broken windows. The back door began to rattle, as the occupants of the house struggled with the door. The Frack brothers and Jake took foot and ran at full tilt back toward Joe's and Rob's.

Through the darkness they ran, but as they approached their home there was a commotion. The priests of mayhem dropped and slid into the tall grass about thirty feet from where the Frack's called home. They stared from the cover of the tall grass from the dark, as the trash Joe and Rob had ignited earlier, now blazed in the dark night.

From inside their neighbors house the boys heard a man yell, "What the fuck is that smell?"

Apparently the reek of the dead fish was in full effect and funk was driving the Frack's neighbors out of their house.

A large, stocky man with short blonde hair pushed open the back door to be greeted by the trash fire inferno Joe and Rob had set.

"Holy fuck!", the man said, as he pulled off his jacket and began to ineffectually beat the fire under control.

The two sisters fled the house of fish funk to express surprise and anger to their friend, who was waving his burning jacket around.

One of the sisters with sharp eyes caught a glimpse of a movement of the boys in the tall grass.

The woman began yelling at pointing in the direction of Jake and friends.

"There! Right there! Those motherfuckers! Right there!", the sister named Tera screamed.

Joe's, Rob's and Jake's being experienced at evading pursuers, split and ran three different directions. Joe ran into the field South, toward Carter Court. Jake ran East toward Lee Lane, and Rob West shagged ass back toward the house they had just vandalized and gassed.

Jake was the most exposed as he was running toward the middle of the street near the streetlights. Jake ran onto the next block and cut behind the house on the corner of Stonewall Drive and Lee Lane, before he realized he was not being pursued.

Jake listened from his hiding place and to him it sounded like the sisters and the blonde man were too busy dealing with their trash fire to give chase.

Rob was not so lucky.

The Owen Brothers, alerted by the cries of outrage from their neighbors on both sides, came running out of their back door and Rob nearly ran face first into Tony Owen. Tony was dressed in a long, black cape, under a black Bob Seger t-shirt. Tony's face was painted white with black circles under his eyes. Tony was wielding a solid metal rod with a steel ball on top of it.

"Hey motherfucker!" Tony shouted at Rob with anger.

Darren was grabbing up a baseball bat off his patio. Tony drew the steel rod back to swing it at Rob. Rob seeing this stumbled as he tried to reverse course. Tony swung at Rob. Rob bolted in the opposite direction, then Tony pursued his prey.

Meanwhile Jake had doubled back along Stonewall Drive to cut between the Owen's house and the Frach's house.

Rob tried to run into the field and into the darkness, but was cut off by Darren Owen, Tony's younger brother. Rob fast of foot cut back as a running back might and bolted toward the same opening Jake was coming to. Tony saw the direction Rob intended to run and intercepted Rob. Rob made it about half way between the two houses, before Tony caught up to him, and swung his metal rod at Rob.

Jake rounded the corner just in time to see the arc of Tony swing connect with the side of Rob's head. Rob stumbled backward and landed against the brick wall of the Owen's house near Tony's bedroom window. Jake heard the sound of glass break as Rob fell against the brick wall.

Jake moved toward Tomy to use his staff to deflect the blow that was coming toward Rob again. Rob raised his hands to shield his head from the coming blow. At the moment Darren appeared from the darkness and ran directly at Jake with his baseball bat raised. Jake stepped away from Tony and swung his staff to parry Darren's bat.

Jake's staff connected with Darren's bat with a clanking noise. Jake slid his staff over Darren's bat, and turned his staff in a circular motion. Darren's bat was pushed to the ground and Darren pitched himself forward, and rolled over Jake's staff releasing his bat. Jake ran toward Darren, but much to Jake's surprise, Darren jumped up and continued to run toward Stonewall Drive and down the street.

Behind Jake, he heard a bottle shatter, as he turned to see what happened, Rob ran toward him holding his head.

"Come on!" Rob said to Jake.

Jake glanced back between the houses to see Tony holding his head in his hands, as he stumbled into the darkness.

Jake ran after Rob. Jake was almost to the street, when Jake noticed that from under Rob's robe his pants were smoking.

Chapter 7 "The Rumble"

Rob ran while holding his head in his hands. Rob travelled West on Stonewall Drive and Jake chased after him. The street was littered with broken eggs, smashed pumpkins and beer bottles, some broken, some still intact. Near the intersection of Stonewall Drive and Lee Lane Jake looked back over his shoulder and noticed neither Tony or Darren were chasing them.

"Rob! Slow down! Tony and Darren are not behind us." Jake shouted, while huffing and puffing.

Rob kept on running. Jake decided there might be a more important issue he needed to share with his friend.

"Rob, stop! Your pants are on fire!" Jake said.

Rob slowed down, turned around, but continued running, as he ran backwards.

"What?" Rob said and looked down.

"I think Cheech and Chong are smoking out in your underwear!" Jake said, pointing to the smoke pouring out from under Rob's robe.

"Oh shit!" Rob said.

"No, no!" Rob repeated.

Rob ripped his robe aside and grabbed both sides of the fly of his cargo pants and ripped them open. There was a series of pops while the buttons ripped free of the fly and then fell to the street.

Rob stumbled and struggled as he fought frantically to escape from his pants.

"Fuck, fuck, fuck, motherfucker, fuck!" Rob yelled in a panicked voice as he nearly fell over.

FiOweny he was free of his pants.

Rob's dark, blue pants lay crumpled in the street smoking, as Rob stood in the middle of Stonewall Drive in his tidy whities, a dark blue t-shirt, and white Converse High Top All Stars. Both sides of Rob's robe were pushed back over his shoulders.

To Jake, Rob resembled a special needs super hero.

Rob was free of his pants, however there was another serious problem, smoke was rising off Rob's right leg.

It was at that moment Rob took note of his predicament.

"Oh, oh! No, shit, no… fuck!" Rob waved his hands at his leg, but did not dare to touch it. Rob peered down at the beer bottles on the street. He hopped over to four, or five bottles grouped together and grabbed up a couple of half full bottles of Miller Lite. Rob poured both the bottles over his thigh and down to his heel. The smoking stopped, and Rob wiped the liquid from his leg with fast hands.

Rob let out a long breath, as he stood in the street for a moment.

A mother glared at Rob. She walked with her three costumed children as they approached him. Jake stood about a safe distance from Rob appraising him.

As the mother walked past Rob, she asked, "Who in the hell are you supposed to be, boy?"

The woman continued to stare at Rob with clear disdain as she passed him by.

Rob seemed to be about to say something, when his discarded pants burst into flames.

"Nope! Nope! Nope!" Rob began to utter as he walked toward his burning pants, then he began to kick them gingerly toward the rain gutter.

Jake could hear the sound of crunching glass, and bottles clinking together. There were clearly four or five more concoctions in the unbroken bottles in Rob's flaming pants. Suddenly Jake heard a loud,oily sizzling sound and a high pitched whistling sound coming from the heap of burning pants and bottles Rob was kicking.

"No! NO! NO! NO!" Rob began to shout with alarm in his voice.

Jake took four or five huge steps away from Rob.

Rob covered his face with his arms as he continued to push the burning pile toward the gutter grate. Something was pouring out of the heap and leaving a fire trail, which Rob was walking directly through, hyper focused on the task of getting the burning payload into the gutter. The bottles made a clanging noise as they slid across the gutter's metal grate.

Now Jake could hear a gurgling sound, as Rob kicked the fiery mess toward the hole at the curb.

"Oh fuck! OH FUCK! FUCKTY FUCK FUCK!", Rob shouted.

The burning heap jammed in the hole for a moment, but after three light, panicked taps from Rob's shoe the burning concoctions dropped into the gutter. Rob stepped from the gutter, as some small, oddly colored, magenta flames leaped up through the gutter's metal grate.

Then it was quiet, as Rob stood there looking at the gutter.

Then a loud rumble shook the street under Rob's and Jake's feet. Seven foot flames shot out of the gutter's mouth. The air sizzled and crackled leaving a haze of green acidic smoke. Half a block away on Stonewall Drive, a manhole cover was blown three feet into the air, as an orange plume of fire shot out around it into the night sky.

Down the street the mother with the trick or treaters grabbed up one of her children, as the family screamed and ran away from Rob and the commotion.

Jake looked Westward on Stonewall Drive as the manhole cover crashed to the street and a huge white ring of smoke was pushed up from the manhole.

Rob stood in the middle of the street, then walked over to the gutter and carefully peered down into the gutter's grate. At that moment, the gutter belched out a huge, yellow flame into the air burning off Rob's eyebrows and the bangs of his hair.

Jake watched as Rob flailed his hands in front of his face. Rob seemed to either be fighting off some unseen demon, or possibly warding off some unseen fire, Jake was no longer sure, and was almost certain he was in shock. Another quake shook the ground under Jake's feet. Jake grabbed onto a black, greasy telephone pole. Rob stumbled in the street, trying to keep from falling down.

Jake stood there holding the broad, telephone pole. He could feel
the pole continuing to vibrate against his body. Jake held the pole
until it stopped vibrating, he let it go.

Jake looked over at Rob. Rob was standing in the middle of the
street again. Rob reached into his shirt pocket and pulled out his
pack of Winston Light cigarettes, shook one out, grabbed it, then put
it in his mouth. Rob was patting his thighs where his pockets would
be, if he was not standing in the middle of the street in his
underwear.

It was at that point Jake noticed Rob's cape was burning at the
bottom.

"Rob, you're on fire again.", Rob said, dazed.

"Oh?" Rob said, turning his head to look behind him at his burning
cape.

"Oh, good." Rob said, as he grabbed his robe, and lifted the burning
cloth up to his cigarette. Rob lit his cigarette, as drops of the
melting viscose burned and dripped to the street.

"Thanks, Jake." Rob said evenly, as he tried to shake and pat the fire
on his burning robe out.

Chapter 8 "The Premonition"

Joe walked into the middle of Stonewall Drive in front of the Frack's
house. He looked West to where Rob and Jake stood in the street,
as they tried to collect their bearings.

"What the fuck was that?" Joe yelled to Rob and Jake.

Rob turned to Joe, as he snapped out of his daze. Rob shook his head and began walking toward his house and Jake followed him. As Rob neared Joe, Joe looked at Rob's pale, naked legs and his white Fruit of the Looms.

"Where the fuck are your pants?" Joe said laughing at Rob.

As Rob got close to Joe, Joe said, "Where the fuck are your eyebrows?"

As Jake got closer to Rob, Jake noticed Rob was bleeding from the back of his hairline.

"Rob?" Jake called to Rob.

"Am I on fire again?" Rob asked.

"No, you're bleeding from your head." Jake answered.

As Rob walked past Joe, Rob placed his hand on the back of his head, then looked at the palm of his hand.

"Fuck!", Rob said looking at his blood covered palm, as he walked past Joe and between the Frack's house and the Owen's house.

As Jake walked toward Joe, Joe asked, "What is wrong with him?"

Jake looked at Joe incredulously, and said, "Rob has a concussion, almost certainly shell shock, but worst of all, he is Rob."

Joe and Jake followed Rob to the back of the Frack's house. Rob walked into the backyard and began looking for something.

"Are you looking for your pants or your eyebrows?", Joe asked as he walked over to his brother.

"What?" Rob said with his cigarette hanging out of the corner of his mouth.

An intuition had been building in Jake's mind. His mind had been making a calculation of the cumulative consequences of Joe's, Rob's and his own actions and began to anticipate an inevitable reckoning in Jake's near future.

In the peaceful quiet, as Jake stood in the darkness, listening to his ears ring, and as Rob, and Joe bickered in their dark backyard, a revelation came to Jake in the form of a premonition. Jake suddenly felt an overwhelming foreboding feeling that told him to take his Shaolin Monk costume off right now!

Jake began to remove his robe and mini cape as he walked over to where Joe and Rob were searching for something in their backyard.

As Joe walked toward Rob, Joe's foot slammed into something hard.

"Fuck god damn motherfucker son-of-a-bitch!" Joe cried out.

"There it is!" Rob beamed, as he bent over to pick up the bowling ball he had thrown out the back door earlier.

Jake had just finished folding his robe, mini cape and belt. He walked over to the Frack's shed and placed his folded up costume into the Frack's shed.

"Jakey-boy, come here." Rob said.

Jake walked over to Rob.

"Here, take this." Rob said, handing Jake the bowling ball.

"Christ, how much does this weigh?" Jake moaned.

"Sixteen pounds." Rob said, as he pulled open the door to the shed and pushed it against the side of his house.

"Give me a hand, Joe?" Rob asked.

"Give me head?" Joe replied, but walked over to where Rob was beginning to scale the support beams on the shed door.

As Rob braced himself with one arm on the top of the shed door and the other on the roof. Joe grabbed one of Rob's feet and helped push him up, as Rob climbed on top of the roof of his house. Next Joe scaled the door and Rob offered Joe a hand up. Joe grabbed it and crawled up onto the roof.

Rob walked over and stood on the roof's edge and said, " Okay Jake, now throw me up the bowling ball."

Jake tried to decide whether pitching underhanded, or passing the ball up like a basketball would work better. Jake decided that underhanded was the better way to heave the ball up to Rob. Jake bent his knees and held the ball between his legs with both hands, and looked up at Rob.

"Okay, are you ready?" Jake asked Rob.

Rob stood precariously close to the roof's edge and peered down at Jake, as Rob stood there he began to wobble.

"Okay, which one of you is going to throw the bowling ball?" Rob said, slightly slurring his words.

Joe walked up beside Rob, and pushed Rob back and out of the way.

"Go over there." Joe instructed Rob pointing somewhere behind him.

"Okay, Jake throw me that heavy motherfucker." Joe instructed.

Jake knew they wanted to get this job done on the first try. Jake did not want to heave the heavy ball in the air only to lose sight of it in the night sky, then have sixteen pounds of urethane come back down and crush his skull.

"Ready?" Jake asked, looking up at Joe.

"On three?" Joe replied, looking at Jake's apprehensive expression.

"On three." Jake confirmed.

Joe and Jake counted together.

"One, two and three", they counted and Jake threw the bowling ball up as he swung his arms and pushed his knees up.

The ball flew up to Joe, who caught the ball with his arms extended out in front of him. As Joe took hold of the ball, his balance shifted forward and he began to pitch forward and off the roof.

Rob groggy, but quick of mind and hands, reached out from behind Joe and grabbed the back of his brother's pants and belt, then fell back into a sitting position on the roof.

Rob was still pulling on the back of Joe's pants and belt. Joe stumbled backward hugging the heavy bowling ball to his chest, as his ass slammed into Rob's face.

"Hey!" Rob jeered, then punched Joe in the ass.

Joe rolled away from Rob laughing.

"I didn't know you cared." Joe said.

"Fag!" Rob jeered at Joe.

"Fag!" Joe Jokingly accused back.

Jake, having scaled the door without assistance, peered over the edge of the roof at the Frack brother's interaction.

"Get a room you two!" Jake said as he heaved himself onto the roof.

Joe shushed Jake. Jake shushed Rob. Rob Shushed Joe. The brother's crawled to the peak of the roof. Jake carefully walked to the roof's peak.

"Jake, get down like this." Joe said.

Jake got down on his stomach and layed on the roof and peered down on Stonewall Drive like Joe and Rob were doing.

"Now that we got that heavy fucking thing up here, what are you going to do with it?" Jake asked.

"Patience Grasshopper, good things come to those who wait." Joe teased.

"Like jail, and brutal beatings by enraged victims?" Jake asked.

Joe and Rob laughed.

"Relax, Jake my man, breathe in that fresh air and take in the beautiful view." Joe said.

Jake noted the air reeked of burnt hair, dead fish, burning rubber, and noxious gases.

Jake surveyed the streets from his discrete rooftop view.

Jake looked West. Smoke was still drifting out of the manhole on Stonewall Drive, where Rob had caused an explosion earlier. Two kids on skateboards were olling over the smoking man hole. Near the corner of Stonewall Drive and Longstreet Drive black smoke was rising from a car that someone had set on fire. For now only the front half of the car was burning.

Closer Jake began to track a group of pre-teens, who were in the middle of the street on the corner of Lee Lane and Stonewall Drive throwing eggs at the house on the corner, where Jake had hidden behind earlier. Suddenly a stocky man with a gun burst out of the door on the left side of the duplex and ran toward the kids. He shouted at them. The kids scattered and ran South on Lee Lane. The angry man stopped in the middle of Lee Lane, took aim and began firing the gun at the kids.

Jake heard tires squeal from West on Grandberry Drive. Jake looked in that direction to see a Rutherford County police car round the corner onto Stonewall Drive. It turned on it's lights and siren, and began to speed toward the man firing the gun. The stocky man stopped firing his gun and ran into the dark field behind his house.

Jake bemused, watched the course of the police car. Between the houses across from the Owen's house, some teens hunkered down, as they launched a barrage of bottle rockets at the patrol car. One of the bottle rockets went in the police car's open driver's side window and exploded inside the driver's compartment. The police car swerved to the right and side swiped a brown station wagon, then kept going.

A moment before they were mangled by the out of control patrol car, some trick or treaters dived off Stonewall Drive and into a yard, as the car sped past them. The Rutherford County Police car sped East on Stonewall Drive, ran over the manhole in the middle of the street, before swerving to avoid the burning car on the corner of Longstreet Drive. The car then turned left, then turned right on Wise Drive and drove toward John Coleman Elementary School.

Across the street from the Owen's house, one of the bottle rocket kids ran out from between the houses, went West on Stonewall Drive. Jake watched as the boy stopped in front of the Gate's house and began to soap the windows on a red 1968 Chevelle. From Grandberry Drive a short, stocky kid with curly blonde hair, ran up East on Stonewall Drive, tackled the kid soaping the car window and began slamming the prankster's head against the street.

Somewhere East of Lee Lane people were shouting and screaming, as two paddy wagons turned left off of Wise Drive and sped in that direction.

"Christ fucking wept." Jake said aloud as his eyes drank in the Boschian hellscape around him.

Beside Jake, Joe and Rob cackled maniacally like demented school boys burning earthworms with exposed electrical wires.

It was hard for Jake to know how much time had passed, since they had scaled the roof. Jake guess thirty, maybe forty five minutes, an hour? He had no fucking idea.

From the South three people rounded the corner on Lee Lane and walked West on Stonewall Drive toward the Frack's house. Joe holding the bowling ball observed the woman was very obese. Joe noted the two men accompanying her were talking loudly, stumbling and appeared to be drunk. Both men were wearing t-shirts with their sleeves cut off and dirty baseball caps. Both men had beer guts, but they were also stocky.

Joe and Rob began laughing. As the three walked through the street, Joe placed the bowling ball in front of him on the peak of the roof and waited for his prey.

Jake listened from the rooftop, as dread gripped his heart. Jake listened to the drunken trio's loud voices in the night.

"Yeah, that's right, Mutherfuckah! That's wut I'm sayin!" one of the men shouted laughing.

To Jake the men looked about forty years old and were probably part time construction workers and full time alcoholics.

"Meryl, you a crazy sum bitch. You know that!" Meryl's friend said.

"Youse boys 're bof crazy, yas hear me!", the big woman with a blonde mullet concurred.

Rob licked his index finger and held it up to test the wind direction.

"Ready?" Bob said quietly to Joe from the rooftop, as Joe posed the bowling ball for release.

Jake was unaware of it, was shaking his head, as he laughed a single laugh of disbelief.

"Don't ya know it? Don't cha, buddy? Jake heard Meryl saying.

"Go." Joe said and released the bowling ball.

The heavy ball thumped loudly as it rolled down the slope of the rooftop. The gutter rattled loudly as the ball rolled over it, then fell. The sixteen pound ball dropped twelve feet and hit the Frack's sidewalk. The impact made a loud sound as it broke the concrete.

The drunken trio in the street stopped and turned to see what the sound was. The two guys flanked the fat lady, as the heavy, black, bowling ball came bouncing down the sidewalk. The lady stared as the heavy, black, bowling ball bounced out the darkness into the street, where she was standing, and it slammed into her left shin.

From the rooftop Joe, Rob and Jake heard the meaty thump.

"Ow, god dammit. Mah leg is broken and I'm pregnant!", the pregnant woman with the mullet screamed.

"Mothahfucker!", Meryl's friend shouted.

"It's ah gawd damn bowlin' ball!" Meryl shouted.

The woman mewled and screamed loudly.

"Who the fuck did that?", Meryl's friend shouted.

Jake hid his head behind the roofed peak as he looked to Joe and Rob. They peered over the roof and laughed.

"Oh fuck." Rob said quietly, as if he had just divined, that reckless actions cause disastrous consequences.

Jake knew it was not going to take long for these people to draw a straight line to figure out where the ball came from. Jake looked down from the roof at the dark field behind Joe's and Rob's house.

"Someone is gonna get their ass kicked!" Meryl proclaimed.

"Frank, Meryl, help me! Aghhhhh!" the woman cried out dramatically.

"Hey, there some motherfuckers 're up on dat roof!" Frank pointed up at Joe and Rob.

"HEY, MOTHERFUCKERS! YOU BROKE MAH WIFE'S FUCKIN' LEG! YOU SON OF A BITCHES!" Meryl yelled.

Minnie stumbled in the street and yelled, "OHHHHHH!"

"Hey man, were sorry man." Rob said to them.

Use the word "man" a few more times and they'll let it go, Jake thought to himself.   Jake tried to calculate in the dark how far it was from the roof to the ground. Fourteen, twelve feet? Enough to break both your legs?

"Motherfuckers, come down here, so I can beat your asses!" Frank demanded.

"Yeah, you fucking pussies! You hit a pregnant woman with a fucking bowling ball! You deserved to get y'alls asses kicked now! Motherfuckers!" Meryl concurred.

"Hey man, it was an accident. You know how it is. We're sorry, man." Joe said, trying to deescalate the situation.

Jake's heart and thoughts raced. He, they, the three of them, were clearly in the wrong by any consideration. Denying any fault and running the fuck away was clearly the right path to take. However if Jake leaped off the house and sprained, or broke his leg, he was in a ripe position for an ass whipping from two muscle bound rednecks and, whoever else decided to join in and beat him to death. Here on the roof, he and his demented friends were in a relatively safe position for the moment, because even if there was fifty, free, bacon cheeseburgers waiting on the rooftop for these tubby bastards, it was unlikely they could get up here.

But Jake thought what if you are wrong? Jake considered leaping to the hard ground in the dark again.

"Too late for sorry, mothefuckers. I'm gonna kick your pussy asses, motherfuckers." Frank threatened angrily.

Joe stood up on the roof looking down on the furious trio and said, "Look man, I live over here."

Joe pointed down to the house next door.

"My name is Tera, Ter... Terry. Terry. Why don't you just come back next week and we will work this whole thing out. I will give you a case of beer and some Weightwatchers." Joe offered.

"HEY, motherfuckers come down here, NOW!" Frank shouted to the boys.

"Frank, Meryl, called the god damn police! We'll haf these mothahfuckers arrested fo' assaulting a pregnant woman! Ohhhhh!", Minnie squalled.

"Come down here, now!", the men shouted together.

Bob stood up beside Joe, both in their robes.

"Look, violence is against our religion." Joe explained, as Rob nodded in agreement.

At that moment a Tennessee State Police car rolled up to where Minnie, Meryl and Frank were standing. The three walked to the police car and began yelling at the officer in the car.

On the roof, the boys looked at each other, and Joe said, "Now."

The three Priests of Mayhem ran down the roof, over the shed and leaped into the uncertain night. Jake hit the ground first and rolled trying to dampen the impact. He rolled five or six times and jumped to his feet. Then Joe a split second later on the hard ground dropped and rolled on his side, then rose to his feet Last Rob hit the ground, tumbled to the ground rolled a few times, tried to get back to his feet, then fell back down then got up again.

Darren Owen was waiting in the shadows behind his house, as the three friends hit the ground.

"Hey!" Darren yelled at the boys.

From between the Owen's and Frack's house, Jake heard someone else yell, "Hey!" as well.

Hearing their pursuers, the three Priest of Mayhem split up, ran toward the dark open field and into the night. Joe ran South toward Carter Court. Bob ran Southwest to cross Carter Court to hide by trees in the next open field. Jake ran West toward the West leg of Stonewall Drive. Darren chased after Jake, but Jake ran between two houses and vanished into the shadows and Darren lost him.

Chapter 9 "The Noose"

Jake was walking North on Lee Lane back toward Stonewall Drive and back towards Joe's and Rob's house. Jake was physically shaking. Jake was certain the police were already looking for him along with Joe and Rob. If the police had already caught Joe or Rob, it was likely they had given him up. And if Joe and Rob had not reported Jake to the police, Tony and Darren probably had. Moreover Jake was pretty damn sure it was after the eleven p.m. curfew.

The air was thick with a haze of smoke from fires. Jake could hear a police siren somewhere close by. Jake walked on the crumbling sidewalk on the West side of Lee Lane. His eyes were searching for police cars. He had seen a few, and two paddy wagons on the prowl, so Jake stayed closer to the houses, than he usually dared to in case he needed to bolt to the dark fields to evade the police.

 Jake's nerves were now beyond fraid. Jake had to walk closer to the houses, which meant Jake needed to be hyper-vigilant for enemies that lurked in the darkness between the houses, especially the Owen brothers. Technically, Jake had done nothing to them, but being attacked for his poor choice of company was a likely possibility, even on the best of days on The Base, let alone in the Dantean nightmare tonight had become.

"Abandon hope all ye who enter here.", Jake said to himself.

As Jake scanned Stonewall Drive, he saw some people walking East on Stonewall Drive and a red headed girl riding a bicycle East. Jake noticed her bicycle was similar to the one he owned. As he looked more closely he realized this resemblance to his bicycle was more than just a passing one.

"Fuck!" Jake said loudly.

It was Jake's bike. There was only one 26 inch, purple Murray, Baja bicycle on The Base, and it was Jake's, and she was riding it.

Jake began to run toward the red headed girl. She was riding East and away from the Frack's house. She was a quarter of a block away, but Jake closed the distance quickly. Jake was prepared to tackle her.

"Hey! Hey! That's my fucking bike!" Jake yelled at her.

As Jake grew nearer, he realized the girl riding the bike was his neighbor, a girl named Lydia.

Lydia turned toward Jake. Lydia was a year older than Jake and they went to the same school. Lydia was a ginger with freckles on her face and body. Her hair was long and straight. Lydia was wearing overalls, with a yellow t-shirt under it, a green flannel shirt over it and she had black Chuck Taylor tennis shoes on her feet.

Jake ran in front of Lydia and stopped her.

"What the fuck are you doing on my bike?" Jake yelled.

"I borrowed it. Cool down. Relax." Lydia said sitting on the bicycle at the intersection of Lee Lane and Stonewall Drive.

"Borrowing without asking and taking my bike out of my shed is called stealing, bitch!" Jake said accusingly.

"Don't call me a bitch!" Lydia sneered back at Jake..

"How about 'thief'?" Jake asked.

"Chill out, Jake. Jesus, I will give you a blowjob to make up for it if you can settle the fuck down." Lydia said, stepping off the bicycle.

Jake was nonplussed for a moment.

Jake looked to Lydia. Despite her tom boy style, she had a nice body. Jake had never been attracted to Lydia before now, but as he viewed her under the streetlight, Jake found her long red, blondish hair, blue eyes and her flirtatious, half smile very attractive.

Lydia cocked her head, as if to say, Well?

"Well, in that case…." Jake paused.

He began to say something, but then Jake looked over Lydia's shoulder. There appeared to be a crowd gathering in the street near Joe's and Rob's house.

"I…." Jake began.

Lydia raised her eyebrows.

Jake noticed Rob was sitting on his porch smoking a cigarette with his robe pulled over his shoulders again. There was a crowd of about twenty people gathering in the middle of the street and Joe was standing inside the group. More people were joining in.

"Excuse me…" Jake said, took his bicycle from Lydia, stepped on to it and rode toward the group.

Lydia followed behind Jake.

Jake cut to the left of the group and slowly began to circle it. Jake's ears were keen, as he had been on edge all night. As Jake rode he listened to and watched the crowd.

"There were three of 'em." A man close to the center said, but Jake could not see him, or see who he was.

"Yeah, one of them sum bitches hit mah wife in the leg with a fuckin' bowlin' ball!" Meryl said.

FUCK! Jake thought as panic began to assail him.

"OHHHHH! It hurts, Ay can barely walk!", Minne moaned.

Jake looped around the crowd again listening with mounting apprehension.

"What a bunch of assholes!" Jake heard Joe shout from within the crowd.

"Yeah!" four, or five of the mob agreed.

SHIT! Jake thought, still listening and circling the mob at a bit faster speed.

"What did they look like?" a guy asked.

"They were dressed like Shaolin monks." Darren Owen answered.

"I chased one of them, but he got away." Darren continued.

Jake ducked down on his bicycle as he rode.

"They deserve to get their asses kicked!" another member of the crowd offered, as he drew sounds of agreement from many of the others.

"Yeah!" Joe concurred laughing.

Jake shook his head as he listened. His heart was beating fast, and seemed to be trying to beat it's way out of Jake's chest.

"We already reported their asses to the cops and they are looking for the three of them." Frank said.

"They are probably the ones, who busted out my window and gassed us out of our house!" jeered a man standing next to an older woman.

The man's words drew grumbles of sympathy from the crowd.

Jake's breath stopped as he recognized them as the husband wife or son mother couple, whose house Joe and Rob attacked earlier.

"Two of them fucked my wife!" Joe confided to the crowd.

This drew sounds of disgust from several of the mob.

"That is nothing! That dumb ass almost blew up half of the block!" The mother of the trick or treaters said, as she pointed to the Frack's stoop.

The eyes of the angry mob turned toward the Frack's house. Sitting on the concrete stoop was Rob Frack. Rob had the side of his burnt and torn robe over his shoulders like a cape. He had his legs spread, offering the lynch mob a view of his nuts encased by his tight, white underwear. A cigarette dangled from the corner of his mouth. The remains of his bangs were singed and stood straight up on his scalp. Rob raised his eyebrow-less brow, smiled and waved to the enraged mob.

Just then there was a commotion as Tony Owened pushed his way to the center of the crowd.

"That ain't shit! Look at what that son of bitch did to my shirt." Tony said as he grabbed a handful of his Bob Seger and the Silver Bullet Band concert shirt.

Jake's stomach dropped away as he looked at Tony Owen. Jake slightly swerved involuntarily as he stared.

Tony's shirt had turned green and appeared to be disintegrating where Rob had thrown his concoction on it.

"And look at your fucking hair!" a little girl said, pointing at Tony's head..

Tony reached up to touch his long, curly hair, as a large chunk of it came off in his hand. Much of Tony's hair had already fallen out from several areas on his head. Most of the hair that remained appeared to have turned to something resembling white straw that stood straight up on his head. The brittle strands of Tony's hair rustled and broke as Tony ran his hand over it.

"Noooo!", Tony moaned as his immediate shock turned to anger.

"Damn!" a young boy said, as Tony's hair fell to the ground.

"You MOTHERFUCKER! I AM GOING TO KILL..." Tony spit, as the angry crowd turned toward the Frack's stoop.

Where Rob Frack was just a moment ago, there was nothing, but a half smoked cigarette smoldering on the broken sidewalk.

Jake drifted a little further East on Stonewall Drive and into the darkness before he began to loop back. Jake's heart felt like it was in his throat.

"I'm calling the goddamn cops!" Tony said angrily, and stomped toward his house, as Darren, his brother followed behind him.

"Who are the other two? What do the other two look like?" Jake heard an angry voice in the crowd demand.

Jake wanted to bolt right then, but he knew he would draw the crowds attention, and he would give himself away. Jake struggled to not hyperventilate.

The eyes of the crowd searched the crowd and around the street, as Jake drifted into the darkness with his back to the crowd, before circling back toward them.

"One of them is kind of tall and thin with blonde hair." Someone said, as Jake's heart stopped.

"In fact he kind of looks like this guy." a man said and pointed to Joe.

The crowd's eyes turn to Joe.

"He must be one ugly motherfucker then!" Joe said laughing.

Many in the crowd burst into laughter.

"We'll catch that son of a bitch too!" Meryl said.

"There was one more." Jake heard a man say in an angry voice.

Jake turned West as he arcked around the lynch mob in a long oblong circle, like a noose that might soon be around Jake's neck.

"He was tall, and thin." the man continued.

Jake cut back and gave the crowd a wide berth, as angry eyes searched the crowd and the street.

Jake cut West on Stonewall. He picked up speed as he drifted past the crowd again.

"He had long blondish, and red hair…." Jake heard the man say, as Jake sped toward the darkness.

"HEY, is that…" was the last thing Jake heard as he bolted into the blackness of the street, as Stonewall Drive curved South.

Jake pumped the bicycle's pedals as hard as he could. Jake's long blonde hair and red flannel shirt blew out behind him in the night. Jake soared down the broken, potholed street at thirty-five miles per hour. He leaned his head forward as he cut through the darkness. Adrenaline flowed through his veins, his heart pounded, as Jake was immersed in the moment with one single goal, get home! Jake had no other idea of what to do.

Just as Jake came up on Cleaborne Drive, he spotted a cop driving down Cleaborne Drive toward him. As Jake crossed the intersection of Stonewall Drive and Cleaborne Drive, the police car's blue lights, and sirens came on. Jake heard the police car's engine rev faster.

 Jake pushed himself to go faster than he ever had before. His parent's yard was only two hundred feet away, but if the cop saw him enter it, his parent's yard might, as well be five hundred miles away, because all was lost.

Jake bunny hopped his bike over the curb and into the neighbor's yard. He cut close to the neighbor's house and shot like a bullet between the two trees leading to his parent's yard. Jake locked up the bicycle brakes and slid into his parent's carport between the shed and his father's station wagon without scraping it's paint job.

Jake heard the police car's sirens and engine speed past his parents house on the other side of the shed. The car screeched to a halt as it stopped at the intersection of Stonewall Drive and Mitchell Drive. Jake sat still in silence.

Jake heard the police car's tires squeal again as the car turned. Jake waited. As he heard the sirens get quieter. Jake knew the police car had turned right on Mitchell Drive and was speeding West and away from him.

Jake sat in the dark silence for a brief eternity, and tried to calm himself down to collect his thoughts. Jake looked toward the carport screen door that led to the kitchen. Jake knew it would be locked, as would be the wooden door with a dead bolt. Jake did not have a key. The lights in the house were out and Jake knew his parents were in bed. Jake would have to wake his parents.

Jake needed to get his story together. It would not be unbelievable for Jake to say that he and the Frack brothers had had an argument and Jake decided to come home. Jake had had falling outs while visiting friends, whose house he was staying over at, and he had returned home. Kids fight.

Jake's parents would be pissed about him waking them up, but it would not be the first time, or the second, or the third... Jake would want to avoid ANY conversation about the ACTUAL events that led to him coming home, so Jake needed to be as quiet as possible as he put his bicycle into the shed, where it was before Lydia stole it. Jake cringed, because he knew his father was easily awakened, especially by noises from his shed.

Jake quietly, without light, opened the shed door. The hinges creaked.

Fuck! Jake thought.

Jake somehow managed to avoid bumping his bicycle into the walls or any random tools scattered on the floor, as he slipped his bike into his father's shed. A small fucking miracle, Jake thought, as his heart continued to pound.

 Jake walked around the shed door to it's hinges and spit on them, then shut the door silently.

Okay, now calm the fuck down, before you have to deal with your parents.

Jake breathed deeply and regained some measure of calm.

Somewhere not far away Jake heard police sirens.

Jake walked around the back of his father's station wagon and up to the carport door. Jake raised his hand to knock on the screen door, when his heart froze in his chest. Jake realized he had made a monstrous mistake and it was probably already too late to do anything about it.

Chapter 10 "The Wire"

Jake needed to get away from here, because he was standing in the last place he should be and about to do the worst thing he could do. In the middle of the angry mob would be worse, but Jake was where they would come for him once they figured out who he was along with the police.

Jake froze for a moment. The panicked child inside Jake's mind begged for his parent's comfort and protection, but the budding pragmatic inside of Jake knew once his father discovered what Jake had done Jake Sr. would help the mob beat his ass, then hand Jake over to the police.

Jake forced himself to move to the edge of the carport. Jake leaned against the wall and peered North up Stonewall Drive, the way he had just come from. Jake held his breath as his heart pounded in his chest. He looked to see if the enraged mob was stomping down the street with torches, pitchforks and rope in hand, ready to welcome Jake as the guest of honor at a good ole fashion, Southern lynching.

Jake needed to stay the fuck off the roads and out of sight. Jake was about to bolt when he saw headlights coming down Stonewall Drive toward him. From Jake's elevated vantage point, he could tell the car was probably still almost a quarter of a mile away. However, if the car was a police car and the patrolman caught a glimpse of Jake crossing his yard, Jake was fucked.

Even if Jake managed to evade the cop, the police would know Jake, who was a almost certainly wanted by this point as a suspect for committing vandalism, assault, arson, malicious mischief, destruction of Federal property and possibly attempted murder for trying to gas a possible mother and son couple ...and oh yeah, being out after curfew.

FUCK! Jake shouted in his mind.

The car continued to come toward Jake.

And hell yes, it's a fucking a Ruthforrd County Patrol car, Jake thought, as it passed under the street light.

 If it was possible for a thirteen year old in nearly perfect health to have a heart attack, Jake would have been dead.

Jake knew when the police figured out who he was, they would come here and Jake was all but certain that was this Rutherford County Patrol car, that was coming to his house for him.

Near Cleaborne Drive the lights on top of the car lit up and the siren blared. Jake was sure the cop had made his position and Jake wanted to bolt, but something held him in place, then Jake's intuition was confirmed, as he watched the cop car make a hard, right turn on Cleaborne Drive.

Jake let out his breath in the darkness.

Jake moved into the yard, not running, but moving fast, away from his parent's house, before another fucking pig drove by, before his parents woke up, before the police showed up to question Jake's father about Jake's whereabouts tonight, before a blood thirsty mob showed up to draw and quarter him, before the god damn sky fell on his head and killed him… Jake was getting the fuck out of here.

"Getting the hell out of Dodge." Jake said quietly, skulking West through his neighbors yard.

Jake crouched down as he walked, staying close to the tree line that separated the properties.

Jake moved parallel to Cleaborne Drive behind rolls of houses.

Where Cleaborne Drive began to curve to the North there was an opening where a house had once been. Though Jake was about a hundred feet away from the street, Jake could hear glass shattering, as some people threw objects through the windows of a house on the Northside of Cleaborne Drive.

Jake moved to the Southside of the tree line of the properties, as he continued to sneak north. Through the windows of the vandalized house Jake could see the house beginning to catch fire.

Jake knew this would draw the police. He fled up the hill, as the houses on his left gave him cover again.

Fucking hell, Jake cursed silently as the thoughts in his brain squirmed from stress.

Jake knew he needed to get back to Joe's and Rob's as soon as he could. It was a bad plan, but it was the only one he had.

Sure I could flee the state, Jake thought.

This could be a shining opportunity to run away from my abusive parents, Jake thought.

He had been giving this idea some serious consideration long before this hellish night.

But first I need to talk to Joe and Rob to find out how much trouble I am in, before I can begin to plan what comes next, Jake thought.

Jake's attention was brought back to the hot, frightening now, as a small group of dogs began to bark frantically from behind a house located near, where Cleaborne Drive intersected with Lee Lane.

There was an abandoned playground in the tall weeds with a tall swing set. Jake bolted for it, as Jake listened for the sound of running dogs.

Stray dog packs were common on The Base, so were people, who just let their vicious dogs run around and attack strangers, especially at night.

Jake looked for a stick on the ground he could use as a club, but he could not see shit in the tall weeds in the dark.

Jake entertained the idea of trying to climb one of the supports of the swing set.

And wait there until the police come and get you? Jake thought to himself bitterly.

Jake knew he might be able to kick one or two medium size dogs to death or at least into retreating. Jake had ran over attacking dogs on his bicycle, and used sticks to beat them into a retreat during the day. ... but here in the dark, and if there were three, four or five? The dogs would out flank him and bite his hamstrings, then he would fall and they would chew his hands and face off.

As Jack approached the swing set, he heard the dogs feet scampering, but then he also heard them banging against metal. Jake paused long enough to try to climb the swing support to safety to scan the backside of the houses on Cleaborne Drive.

In the blackness Jake could make out a large dog pin with a fence and maybe a corrugated metal fence around some of it.

The dogs barked and banged on the fence, but they seemed to be contained. So far.

"Fuck you Cujo." Jake cussed, angrily in the dark.

I will feed you some tasty steak and clock parts at my earliest inconvenience, Jake considered.

Jake began to move silently and carefully back to the tree line.

There was a trail that cut through between Cannon Drive on the Southside of the treeline and ran to the Cul De Sac on Longstreet Drive, as Jake approached it he heard some men talking as the trees rustled ahead of him.

Silently Jake dropped to the ground and hid in the tall weeds and waited.

Jake needed to get to the woods, which were on the other side of the trail. Jake's plan was to get to the woods, navigate the trails that ran parallel to the houses on Longstreet Drive in the pitch black night. From the woods, Jake would try to find a safe place to cut through a backyard, then cross Longstreet Drive going West, go between the houses into the dark field, continue West, then cut across over Lee Lane, then cross Carter Court, then cut between the houses into the dark field, then to Joe's and Rob's house without being seen, captured by the police, attacked by enemies, attacked by vicious dogs or random, everyday garden variety crazies that lurk around The Base.

Jake estimated the distance was only between a quarter and half mile of harrowing hellscape to get to the Frack's house, where the police might already be there waiting for him. If so, Jake would be on the run without money or a single ally. It was a totally shit plan, but it was the only one Jake had.

...And yet, there was another problem. As Jake lay in the grass, not fifty feet away two cops walked from the treeline on the trail. ...which Jake would have to cross to get to the woods.

Jake's heart pounded like a sledgehammer, as he explored the possibility of holding his breath while his heart pounded like a fucking sledgehammer.

As Jake lay on his stomach incoherent with fear he tried to will himself to become invisible, as he watched two dark uniformed policemen walk by in front of him.

One of the policemen stopped for a moment.

"Bob, hold on." one of the policemen said to his partner.

The officer scanned the dark field, then he turned his head toward Jake.

"What is that?" the policeman said in a deep voice.

Jake could hear his heartbeat ringing in his ears.

"That!" the policeman said pointing over Jake's body in the dark.

"Is that house on fire?" Bob asked.

"Yep, it is. We need to get back to the car and call it in." Jake heard the other police officer say.

Jake watched as the two policemen walked North toward their police cruiser parked on the cul de sac at the end of Longstreet Drive.

 When their backs were to Jake, he took his first breath in what seemed like forever, as he began to tremble in fear.

Jake's heart hurt as it continued to pound, as he watched the policemen move at a seemingly leisurely pace considering someone's house was fucking burning down.

Take your time, Jake mouthed silently as he watched the men get into their police vehicle, get on the radio, then fiOweny drive away.

Jake began to get up, then paused and listened closely for any foot falls. When he was reasonably certain no one else was near, he slowly crawled on his belly to the treeline.

Slowly Jake rose once he was next to the trees. The woods were about two hundred feet from where he was.

Jake quickly and carefully moved from tree to tree in the dark.

As Jake passed Longstreet Drive, he noticed there was some kind of commotion going on up Longstreet Drive in the direction where he would have to soon cross the street.

Jake reached the woods and ran down the trail. Jake stopped in the dark by a tree and entertained the idea of sleeping in the woods. However Jake knew he had to get to Joe's and Rob's house.

Jake found the trail that cut North. He had not travelled it at night before, but he knew it well enough to find his way. After about five hundred feet and a brief and dark eternity later the trail led into the backyard of the first house on Longstreet Drive after the intersection of Cleaborne Drive.

Jake walked close to the treeline, until he was behind the first house near the intersection.

Jake ran quickly and quietly across the yard. The lights were out on the Northside of the duplex. Jake ran toward the back of the house and skirted along the backside of it.

Jake paused for a moment and tried to guess what time it was as he leaned his back against the coarse brick wall. Twelve a.m.? One a.m.? Jake shook his head. He had no idea. He had lost his ability to track time. He was living in the perpetual, heart attack time of now in this dark forever.

But Jake had to move, before someone in the house came out to find him in their backyard and decided to shoot him. Trespassing was a killing offense on The Base.

"Fucking existing is a killing offense on The Base." Jake said to himself in the darkness.

Jake glanced between the houses on Longstreet Drive, as a paddy wagon drove past.

Sweet Jesus, Jake thought.

Jake knew he had to cross Longstreet Drive and slip between the two houses on the other side. There he might get a brief reprieve as he passed into the dark field between houses, Jake hoped.

"Or I might get shot, beaten up, arrested, or devoured by a wild dog." Jake reasoned pragmatically and fatalistically.

Jake moved in the darkness as he pressed his back against the South wall of the next brick house up Longstreet Drive.

Jake could hear a commotion of people yelling, and something sizzling loudly. Jake poked his head around the corner of the house and looked up the street North.

FUCK! Jake reacted.

There was a paddy wagon in the middle of the street and people were being loaded into it by several cops. There were also people fighting with, and running from the police about two to three houses up the street. Further up the street at the corner of Longstreet Drive and Stonewall Drive, the car that had been burning earlier was now fully ablaze.

 Another police car with its lights on drove past where Jake was still pressed up against the wall in the shadows. Jake heard the police stop as he glanced around the corner.   The car stopped two houses down and the police had gotten out of their car.

Jake knew he needed to move. Every fiber of his being wanted Jake to run. Jake took a breath with his heart in his throat.

He glanced out from behind the corner, ready to run.

Jake saw the two police officers walking toward the next house north of him, when suddenly, there was a huge fiery explosion up the street.

The police turned toward the explosion, as fire rained down from the sky into the street, and on to a large tree on the Westside of the street. Burning debris rained onto the roofs of the houses on both sides of the street.

Jake realized that the fire had fiOweny reached the gas tank of the car he had seen burning earlier from Joe's and Rob's roof.

Jake said a silent prayer to any god that might protect foolish teenagers who hung out with dangerous assholes, then he bolted to the street.

As Jake ran to the street, he soaked in the view, as his panicked mind processed the horrific scene.

All hell had broken loose.

Fire rained down from the sky.

The police who were forcing the arrested into the paddy wagon, now tried to force their way into the holding cells to seek shelter from the burning sky.

A forty foot tree half way up the block was burning, yet people ran under it to shield themselves from the burning, falling fuel and pieces of the exploded car.

Jake saw those, who continued in their anarchy despite the fact the world around them was burning.

A woman was silhouetted in the plume of the giant rising flame. She seemed to be howling as she smashed a police car's window with a tire tool.

A man hurled a cinder block with both hands through the bay window of a house on the East side of the street.

Jake could hear the fire at the intersection up the road making a terrible howling noise as the inferno blazed.

As Jake crossed the middle of the street, running full tilt, he saw a burning tire and rim fall from the heavens and crashed down on top of the paddy wagon, as the police around it dived from it to take cover.

Jake's foot stepped onto the crumbling sidewalk, as people turned away from the exploding bomb that once was a car.

As Jake crossed the Northside of the yard of the first house on Longstreet Drive and ducked between the first and second house, Jake heard someone say, "Hey, there's that..."

Then Jake was in the darkness of the field. He cut right diagoOweny as he ran Northeast, but when Jake saw he was not alone, he dived to the ground in the darkness.

Near the center of the field Jake laid on his stomach again.

All thought of being chased vanished from Jake's mind as he stared North. There were a group of at least six cops in a semicircle pointing their guns at the back door of a house. It was where the man lived who had been shooting at the kids, who had vandalized his house.

The police were shining a light on the back door of the man's house.

From his position in the dirt, three hundred feet away, Jake could hear the police talking among each other and shouting at the man inside.

The police seemed to be focused on the light shining on the backdoor, and they seemed to be about to break the door down.

Jake looked to the opening between the second and the third house on Lee Lane that led to the street. Jake consider crawling the sixty feet from where he was, but he did not want to movement on the ground to draw the police's, or god forbid a fucking dog's attention.

Jake jumped up and ran toward the cover between the two houses. As Jake ran through the darkness, he heard gun fire erupt from the North end of the field.

Jake's heart stopped, but his feet continued to move.

Jake kneeled down for a moment in the darkness, as he leaned against the South wall of the third house.

Jake heard yelling and running on the street.

Jake glanced around the corner.

It appeared there were three police cars, there were police with guns drawn storming the house.

Jake took his chance and ran across the road without looking down the street towards the police. Whatever happened next happened.

In a flash Jake was across the street. He bolted between the two houses and hid in the dark field between Carter Court and Cleaborne Drive by the trees Rob had hidden earlier that night.

Jake sat there for a brief moment. His heart was still in his throat and adrenaline was coursing through his veins.

Jake picked his spot to run to. He knew the path in his mind. Between the first and second houses, then straight across Carter Court, then between the house on the corner of Lee Lane and the first house on Carter Court.

Jake could feel his heart beating in his head. Jake took several deep breaths, as butterflies fluttered in his stomach. Jake had less than one block between him and sanctuary. About five hundred feet.

Jake took off running. He bolted through the space between the two houses in front of him, as a cold sweat ran down his neck.

Four hundred feet to go, Jake thought.

Jake was a blur in the night as he scampered across the cracked and broken asphalt of Carter Court.

Somewhere as he crossed the street Jake heard a quick succession of six gunshots echo through the night air.

Jake broke for the opening between the house on the corner of Lee Lane and the first house on the Northside of Carter Court.

Jake took flight as he leaped over the cracked sidewalk and ran over the dead grass of the yard with his shoes barely touching the ground.

Two hundred feet to go.

As Jake passed between the houses, he could fiOweny see the light in the window of the Frack's house. Safety was in sight at last. Jake's heart felt like it might explode, as he found a reserve of energy he did not know existed

Jake's hair blew back behind him, his red flannel shirt blew in the wind. Though it was a cool fifty degrees Jake's body was covered with sweat, as he pointed himself at the backdoor of Joe's and Rob's house.

Jake closed the last one hundred feet, as he cut through the black night air at blinding speed.

Jake hurled himself over the last fifty feet, as he darted through the dark field.

Jake estimated he had thirty feet as he raced toward his salvation.

Jake was twenty feet from...

Suddenly Jake's feet flew out from under him and went straight up in front of him. He was lifted straight up in the air from his neck five and a half feet up, then he landed flat on his back on the hard ground.

Jake's heart was beating harder, than it had ever had before. His blood surged through his body, yet Jake could not breathe as he lay flat on his back.

Jake fought to breathe. Jake made a rasping noise as he tried to draw breath into his lungs. Jake fiOweny managed to draw some small amount of air into his lungs, as he stared up at the tiny, far away stars in the black sky.

Jake realized all at once he had run into the Frack's metal clothes wire and it had pulled him off his feet.

Jake felt his neck. It felt like it was bleeding. Jake slowly brought himself to his feet, as his ability to breathe returned to him.

Suddenly Jake had to piss! Jake needed to piss more than he had ever before in his life!

Jake's whole body trembled, as he stumbled behind Joe's and Rob's shed. Jake's hands shook so badly, that it was a herculean task to unbutton, unzip his pants, pull his underwear down, find his dick and get it out of his pants to piss.

Once Jake's dick was free in the cold night air, piss jetted from his dick in a fat stream that strained the capacity of Jake's urethra.

Jake pissed for a solid five minutes, as steam rose from the ground in the darkness.

When Jake was finished his body continued to tremble as Jake struggled to zip up and button his pants.

Jake stumbled toward Joe's and Rob's back door. Jake wobbled as he stepped up onto the backdoor stoop.

Jake realized he was seeing stars in his vision. He realized his head hurt. He must have slammed his head on the ground, when he almost killed himself by running into the goddamn clothes wire.

Jake knocked on the backdoor of Joe's and Rob's house. After an eternity of moments, Jake knocked again.

Jake could hear the sound of a T.V. inside the house. The light was on.

A few moments later, Ellen Frack's voice came through the door.

"Who is it?" Ellen said in a grumpy voice.

"It's Jake, Jake Baker." Jake said, trying to speak loud enough for Joe's and Rob's mother to hear him, which was a struggle considering he had about crushed his larynx a few minutes ago.

Ellen Frack pulled back the yellowing window curtain on the door's window and looked at Jake, as she flicked on the back porch light blinding Jake.

"What do you want?", Ellen asked Jake.

I want that Dan Aykroyd pussy! Let me in, bitch!, Jake thought, then said, "I am spending the night with Joe and Rob", as he coughed.

Ellen Frack opened the door and Jake came stumbling into the Frack's house coughing and trembling.

As Jake walked through the cluttered dining room, Joe rose from an easy chair and turned to Jake.

Joe smiled at Jake, but his expression turned to concern as he noticed Jake's entire body shaking.

"Jakey-boy are you okay? You look pale and shook up." Joe inquired.

Jake coughed and struggled to speak.

"Where did you vanish to? Do you need a cigarette?" Joe offered, shaking a Winston from his pack.

With a shaking hand Jake took a cigarette from Joe's pack and put it in his mouth.

Joe handed his green disposable Bic lighter to Jake.

Jake sat down in Joe's chair in the living room, as he struggled to light his cigarette with his shaking hands. Jake's hands were shaking in different directions and the cigarette and the lighter's flame just kept missing each other.

Joe grabbed a kitchen chair and sat down across from Jake. Joe took Jake's hands and pushed the lighter's flame under Jake's cigarette.

Jake's Winston flared a flame as Jake drew deeply on the cigarette.

"Thank you." Jake said to Joe.

"So what happened to you?" Joe asked.

Jake began his story with his interaction with Lydia and finished up with his near hanging, before he arrived at Joe's back door.

As Jake finished he asked the question that would define his future from then on, "So how much trouble am I in?"

"You're fine." Joe replied.

"What the fuck are you talking about?" Jake asked in utter confusion.

"You are in the clear. Nobody could figure out who you were." Joe answered and smiled.

Jake took a handful of his long blonde, red hair and said, "With this? Who the hell else has hair like this?"

"The lady, who got hit with the bowling ball, the two guys, and the mother with the trick or treaters looked around the crowd, and they tried to blame Lydia, the girl you were talking to." Joe said laughing.

"What?" Jake said, as he felt the weight of a thousand bricks of lead lift from his shoulders.

"Yeah, but Lydia gave them a pretty serious rebuke." Joe said.

"Really?" Jake said, letting out a deep breath.

"She was pissed." Joe said, continuing to laugh.

"So I am in the clear?" Jake asked Joe in disbelief.

"You're fine, Jakey-boy" Joe said and smiled at Jake.

Jake felt so relieved, he felt like he was floating on the air.

Jake closed his eyes for a moment, smiled and savored the feeling of relief.

Jake suddenly opened his eyes and blinked, as a question entered his mind.

"What about Rob? Did he get arrested?" Jake asked.

"No, Rob is in the hospital. He had to get seventeen stitches where Tony had hit him in the head and he has a concussion. They are keeping him overnight for observation, but they said he should be fine." Joe replied.

"But what about the police?" Jake asked.

"Ellen told them, Rob has not lived here in a year. After they left she took Rob to the hospital and checked him in under the name Franz Kafka." Joe said and laughed.

"Franz Kafka?" Jake laughed hard and shook his head.

Jake continued to laugh for a long time, then he turned to Joe, smiled and said, "Thanks man."

"For what?" Joe asked.

"For making me feel better. For being my friend." Jake said.

"Anytime." Joe replied and smiled.

"And I have something for you." Joe said to Jake.

"What?" Jake asked with wonderment in his blue eyes.

Joe reached around behind the couch and pulled out Jake's robe, cape, belt and staff.

"I don't have a blanket for you, but…" Joe popped open Jake's robe and handed it to him.

Jake spread the brown robe out over him, laid the mini cape and belt on his chest and leaned the red staff beside him and against the chair.

"They are yours." Joe said.

"Thank you." Jake said, relaxing, as he slouched down into the comfy, easy chair.

"You are welcome, Jakey-boy." Joe said, sitting down on the cluttered couch.

Joe pulled a blanket over his chest and legs and he turned toward the television.

Jake relaxed and closed his eyes and drifted off into deep sleep. Jake dreamed of pleasant things to do on Halloween and waking to the rising sun, that promised a new day that could make even the cracked streets of The Base beautiful.